KIDS CAN'T STOP READING
THE CHOOSE YOUR
OWN ADVENTURE® STORIES!

'It's exciting choosing your own adventure and being the star of the story. It makes you think instead of just reading it and forgetting it'
Charlotte Walton, age 13

'Though I don't like reading much, I loved this'
Robert Gladman, age 10

'I was suffocated twice, buried alive and had a spell put on me – all in one night!'
Karen Hay, age 10

And teachers like this series, too:

'They are very popular and assist in motivating children. Pupils find them absorbing and exciting'
Mr Keith Hurst, Head of English, Frogmore School, Hampshire

CHOOSE YOUR OWN ADVENTURE®
AND MAKE READING MORE FUN!

Bantam Books in the Choose Your Own Adventure® Series
Ask your bookseller for the books you have missed

Sky Lark Choose Your Own Adventure Books for younger readers

THE SECRET TREASURE OF TIBET

BY RICHARD BRIGHTFIELD

ILLUSTRATED BY PAUL GRANGER

An Edward Packard Book

BANTAM BOOKS

TORONTO • NEW YORK • LONDON • SYDNEY • AUCKLAND

To Ann Hodgman

RL 4, IL age 10 and up

THE SECRET TREASURE OF TIBET
A Bantam Book / March 1985

CHOOSE YOUR OWN ADVENTURE® *is a registered trademark of Bantam Books, Inc. Registered in U.S. Patent and Trademark Office and elsewhere.*

Original conception by Edward Packard.

ISBN 0-553-24522-8

Published simultaneously in the United States and Canada

Bantam Books are published by Bantam Books, Inc. Its trademark, consisting of the words "Bantam Books" and the portrayal of a rooster, is registered in U.S. Patent and Trademark Office and in other countries. Marca Registrada. Bantam Books, Inc., 666 Fifth Avenue, New York, New York 10103.

Printed and bound in Great Britain by Hunt Barnard Printing Ltd.

O   0 9 8 7 6 5 4 3 2 1

WARNING!!!

Do not read this book straight through from beginning to end! These pages contain many different adventures you can have while searching for the mysterious valley of Siling-La. From time to time, as you read along, you will be asked to make a choice. Your choices may lead to success or disaster.

Your adventures are the result of your choices. *You* are responsible because *you* choose! After you make a choice, follow the instructions to see what happens next.

Think carefully before you make a move. Any choice could be your last . . . or it *could* lead you to the secret treasure of Tibet.

Good luck!

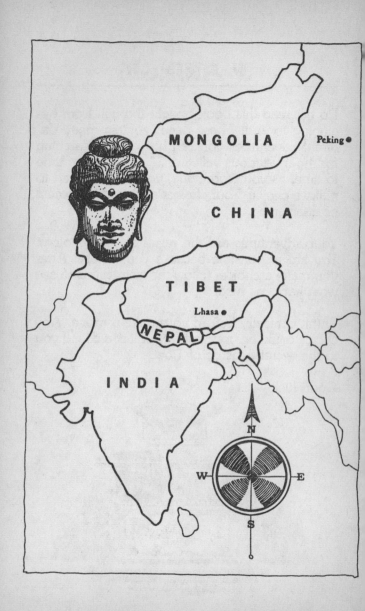

You have just finished a correspondence course on how to be a private investigator. While you are at home one day, wondering what your first case will be, there is a soft knock at your front door.

When you open it, you see an old man standing there.

"Can I help you?" you ask.

"May . . . may I come in?" he says. "There is something I must ask you."

You help the old man to a chair. He sits down with a heavy sigh.

"My name is Bertram Buckingham," he begins. "I got your name from the referral service of your correspondence school. I have a job for you—one that will send you on an adventure beyond your wildest dreams. And all expenses paid, I might add."

"I haven't had much experience yet," you say, "and—"

"That's perfect," Mr. Buckingham interrupts. "I need someone with a young, fresh mind."

"Sounds interesting. Tell me a little about the case," you say, pulling a chair over next to Mr. Buckingham.

Turn to page 2.

"It all goes back many, many years—to 1942, to be exact—during the Second World War," he says. "I was in the British army then, stationed in northern India. I was put in charge of two Germans. They weren't Nazis, but we were holding them until the end of the war. One night they escaped and headed north toward the Himalayas. Since they were my charges, I followed them all the way through Nepal and into Tibet. I lost their trail in a blinding snowstorm, but stumbled into a valley called *Siling-La*. In the midst of snow-covered mountains, it was an almost tropical oasis. Plants and flowers were everywhere. In the center of it was a perfect jewel of a monastery. There I saw an amazing sight—one that has haunted me ever since."

Turn to page 10.

4

You stay in the cab. Soon it pulls up in front of Sylvia Morrison's apartment building, and you get out. The first thing you do is look back to see if the car that was following you is still there. There's no sign of it now. Maybe it was just your imagination, and you weren't being followed at all.

You go into Sylvia's building and ring her doorbell. The door opens a crack, just enough for you to see the woman behind it. She's tall and attractive, with short dark hair and blue eyes. You guess she must be about thirty.

"What do you want?" she asks nervously.

"I'm the one who called you on the phone fifteen minutes ago," you explain.

"I can't talk to you now," she says.

"But it's important that I—" you start.

"All right, then, come in quickly," she says, opening the door.

Turn to page 72.

First you look up Sylvia Morrison's number in the phone book and call her. You introduce yourself and ask her what she knows about levitation.

"That's a big subject," she replies. "I have hundreds of reports on it in my files."

"Would you let me take a look at those files?" you ask.

"I'd be glad to show them to you sometime," she says, "but right now I'm packing for a trip and I don't—"

"In that case, I'll be right over," you say, slamming down the phone.

You throw on your jacket and sprint out of the house. At the corner you hail a cab and give the driver Sylvia Morrison's address.

Halfway there, you notice that another car is following the cab. You wait and watch it for a while to be sure. Why would anyone be following you?

"Driver," you say, "make a sharp right at the next corner."

The cab driver turns. After a few seconds, the other car appears around the corner behind you. Should you keep going to Sylvia Morrison's? Or should you have the cab make another sharp turn and stop so that you can jump out?

If you decide to keep going in the cab, turn to page 4.

If you decide to jump out, turn to page 20.

Quickly you squeeze inside the hollow back of the idol. It's surprisingly roomy inside, as long as you sit cross-legged like the Buddha itself. You feel around the inside with your hand, and brush some kind of lever. There is a swishing sound behind you, and a panel slips into place over the opening—sealing you inside.

You're wondering how you'll ever get out of this when you feel a jolt. Then the statue begins to shake violently.

"Be careful there!" Joe shouts. "This thing is valuable. I don't want any accidents."

You are moving.

As your eyes get used to the darkness inside the idol, you see two tiny pinpoints of light in front of you and above your head. You ease yourself up so that you can put your eye to one of them. You realize suddenly that your head is inside the statue's head, and the points of light must be pinholes in its eyes. You remember that a pinhole can actually act like the lens in a camera and, sure enough, you can see the whole scene in front of you. You are now outside the building and heading for the open back of a large truck. There is another jolt as the idol is slid inside, then darkness again as the doors of the truck are closed.

The truck starts off and continues to move for about an hour. Then it stops. You hear the doors of the truck being opened again.

Turn to page 22.

You freeze on the ledge against the wall of the mansion. The face of a boy—twelve or thirteen years old—appears at the window.

"My name is Jimmy—Jimmy Crossley," he whispers. "Climb into my room. I can help you."

You jump up onto the windowsill and then drop into his room.

"Can you get me out of here?" you ask in a low voice.

"I think so," Jimmy answers. "I've helped other people. Anyway, you'd never make it the way you were going. My father has guards with machine guns, Doberman attack dogs, and—we'll have to wait until morning. Then I'll pretend you're a friend of mine and walk you out the front gate."

Jimmy lends you a blanket, and you spend the rest of the night dozing under his bed—just in case someone comes in during the night.

Early the next morning, Jimmy gets up. "I'll be back after breakfast," he whispers.

When Jimmy returns, the two of you leave his room and head for the wide front steps that lead to the mansion's front door. You and Jimmy are about halfway down the stairs when you see Mr. Crossley approaching.

Crossley, lost in thought, goes right past the two of you. He doesn't even say good morning to Jimmy. But just as you reach the bottom of the stairs, he calls down, "Just a moment there. I'd like to have a word with you."

Turn to page 18.

You go out into the hallway and turn right, toward the door at the end. You've only taken a few steps when you hear voices coming from around the bend in the hallway behind you. Quickly you try a couple of the doors along the side—they're all locked! Now what? Try one more, you think, before making a dash for the door at the far end. Whew! This one opens.

You slip into the room and gently ease the door shut. And just in time! You can hear several men searching in the room where you were tied up.

"I thought you said you had that young snoop tied up in here," one of them says.

"I did, Joe," answers another voice. "I *think* this is the room."

"You think! You think!" Joe exclaims. "All right, we'll figure out what you did later. Right now, we've got to get that statue over to Crossley's place."

Then you hear the men walking toward the room where you're hiding.

Turn to page 15.

10

"What did you see?" you ask Mr. Buckingham.

"The monks there could levitate themselves—you know, rise up off of the ground, and stay there," he answers. "I saw it. They even tried to teach *me* how to levitate, but I still hadn't found the Germans, so I had to continue my search."

"But what's this got to do with today?" you ask.

"I've told this story many times, particularly at my club. Hubert Crossley, another member and a millionaire, has often teased me about it." Buckingham hesitates, looking uncomfortable. "A month ago, in a weak moment, I bet my entire fortune against his. If by this time next year I can't scientifically prove that levitation is possible, then everything I own becomes his. And he has it in writing."

Something tells you your first case isn't going to be easy. "Where do I come in?" you ask.

Turn to page 76.

"I'd love to go to India," you say. "But I'll have to get home in a hurry and start packing."

"Don't worry about that," says Mr. Crossley. "I'm sure we can furnish you with whatever you'll need on the trip."

Suddenly there is a commotion outside. Mr. Crossley moves quickly to the window. While his attention's on whatever is going on in the driveway, you take a close look at the map. There is a large circle penciled in on the upper part of Tibet. And next to it is written: *Siling-La somewhere in this area.*

Then, before Crossley can turn back around, you are at the window beside him. Below, in the driveway, large crates are being carried out of the mansion and loaded into several army-type trucks.

"Ah . . . extra supplies for the trip," says Mr. Crossley as he steers you away from the window and presses a button on his desk.

Turn to page 21.

When you come to, you find yourself tied up in a dark room. Your head is still throbbing from the blow that knocked you out. For a few minutes you just lie there, getting your thoughts together. What did your correspondence course say about freeing your hand when you're tied up? Now you remember—use a slow, steady pull with one hand. Fortunately, there is just enough play in the ropes to squeeze one hand out gradually.

Finally your right hand pulls free. You get your other hand loose and then untie your feet. You stand up shakily, rubbing the large bump on the back of your head.

By now, your eyes are adjusted to the darkness. Far across the room you see the faint, lighted line of the edge of a large door. You walk toward it, stumbling into large crates a few times. You feel around for the doorknob, and are relieved to find the door unlocked.

Cautiously, you open the door a crack and peek out into a wide, brightly lit hallway. No one is in sight, so you slip out into the hall. Nearby, to the left, the hallway rounds a corner. Far down at the other end, to the right, is a closed door that looks as if it might be an exit. There are a number of closed doors on either side of the hallway.

If you decide to go to the right, turn to page 9.

If you decide to go to the left and see what's around the corner, turn to page 101.

14

You get the telephone directory and look up Sylvia Morrison's number. You dial it and a voice answers. The voice is muffled and much heavier than you expected.

"Hello. Is this Sylvia Morrison?" you say. "I'm investigating the phenomenon of levitation."

"Levitation?" she says. "There's not much to investigate. It's really very simple. If you can come over, I'd be glad to demonstrate it for you."

You get dressed and go over to Sylvia's. She doesn't look much like her picture in the paper, but you know that many people use earlier pictures for their publicity photos.

Sylvia offers you some coffee, then sits down cross-legged in front of you. "Levitation just takes concentration," she explains, then closes her eyes.

Keeping your eyes on her, you take a sip of coffee. Almost instantly, your head starts spinning. As you collapse on the floor, you realize there must have been something in the coffee.

Turn to page 87.

You look around. In the dim light the only thing that you can see is a large oriental sculpture, about five feet high and almost as wide at the base, on the other side of the room. It must be an idol, a statue of the Buddha. You hurry over and duck behind it just as the door opens and throws a bright shaft of light into the room.

"That's it by the wall there." You recognize the voice as Joe's. "Let's get a forklift over here. It looks heavy."

As you crouch down behind the idol, you see that there's a large opening in the back of it. It looks as if you could crawl inside. It might be worth a try.

You also notice, however, that the large door of the room opens in. If you could get behind it before the other men get back, there's a good chance that you could hide there.

If you decide to try to squeeze inside the idol, turn to page 7.

If you decide to try to get behind the door, turn to page 78.

The abbot leads the four of you through Siling-La's main temple, then down a narrow stone stairway. The stairs seem to go on forever, winding deep beneath the earth.

Finally, you emerge in a huge cavern. The abbot lights a torch and holds it high overhead. Suddenly, thousands of shining gold objects—statues, bowls, thrones, bracelets covered with gems—flash in its light.

"What you see here is only a small part of the treasure of Genghis Khan," the abbot says softly. "This cavern goes on for miles."

You, Jimmy, von Kamp, and Kurt remain at the monastery for several weeks. You're having a great time, but finally you all agree that it's time to return home.

"I'm afraid that's impossible," the abbot tells you. "Though we are protected, it's best that the outside world forget Siling-La."

"We wouldn't try to take the treasure," Jimmy says.

"Buckingham never even *saw* the treasure," the abbot replies, "yet he brought great danger to many simply by talking about the monastery. We can allow no one to leave."

It's a good thing that you like Siling-La. You're going to be there for a long, long time.

The End

18

"Come up here, will you?" Mr. Crossley calls to you, adding, "Jimmy, wait down there."

Jimmy gives an "I don't know what this is about" shrug with his shoulders as you start back up the stairs. When you get to the top, Mr. Crossley motions for you to follow and leads you down the hallway to a small office.

"Sit down for a moment," he says. He goes to the wall and pulls down a large map.

"Do you know anything about this part of the world?" Crossley asks, sweeping his hand over India and the Himalayas. "I'm taking Jimmy on a month's study tour of the region. It just occurred to me that it might be highly desirable to bring one of his friends along, so he doesn't get lonely. We're leaving tomorrow, and if you're interested—"

"That's kind of short notice!" you say.

"I know it is," says Mr. Crossley, "but I'm confident that we can work out the details if you want to go."

If you decide to go with Jimmy, turn to page 11.

If you decide not to go, turn to page 73.

You follow the man who met Snide. He moves rapidly down the street away from you. You sprint after him, trying to keep to the shadows as much as possible.

Then the man seems to vanish. Cautiously you walk up to where he disappeared. Suddenly you hear a footstep behind you. You turn, but not fast enough. Something very heavy hits you on the back of the head.

Turn to page 13.

You pay the cab driver and tell him to pull around the next corner, wait for a second, then leave as fast as possible.

A minute later, after jumping out of the cab, you press yourself against the shadowed side of a large building. The cab zooms away, and the car following speeds after it. It is a dark blue limousine—one you won't forget.

You set off toward Sylvia Morrison's apartment building. But half a block away, you stop. Ahead, directly across the street from Sylvia's building, is the limousine that followed you.

Carefully you slip into the shadows. Crouching behind a parked van, you see two men—with a woman between them—make their way out of Sylvia's building toward the limousine. As they pass under a streetlight you look at the woman. You recognize her at once from the picture in the paper—it's Sylvia Morrison, and she's in trouble! Her hands are tied behind her back, and the two men seem to be pushing her.

Desperately you try to think of what to do. If you rush out and try to save Sylvia, you could end up a prisoner too. At least you can get the limousine's license plate number.

The two men hustle Sylvia into the car and slam the door shut. The limo pulls away. Quickly you run toward it and start copying the license plate. There are three letters and four numbers: ULO-74—but that's as far as you get. Something hits you on the back of the head, and you lose consciousness.

Turn to page 13.

Almost immediately after Crossley presses the button, a tall man wearing a neatly wound green turban enters.

"This is Narak Singh, one of my servants," says Crossley. "He will see to your needs and drive you to the airport. You will spend the night at the airport hotel. Jimmy will meet you at the terminal. We leave early tomorrow morning."

Singh drives you to your apartment, where you pack a suitcase and get your passport. Singh, however, doesn't let you out of his sight. Two of Crossley's men, in civilian clothes, go along "for the ride."

You spend the night at the airport hotel. The next morning you get your things together and, flanked by Crossley's men, head toward the boarding gate of the Air India flight. The airport is crowded, but not crowded enough to help you if you decide to make a break for it. You can see Jimmy across the terminal floor.

You are about halfway to Jimmy when a large group of vacationers crosses in front of you. You recognize one of them. It's Inspector McElroy, a good friend of your family, and the one who encouraged you to become a private investigator. This may be your chance to get away from Crossley's men—if you want to.

If you decide to use this chance to get away, turn to page 106.

If you decide to keep playing along with Crossley, turn to page 34.

Through the pinholes in the statue's head you can see that you are outside some sort of mansion. A group of men in military uniforms, but without any insignia, are standing behind the truck. What is this all about?

The idol, with you inside, is heaved into the mansion. There you're taken upstairs to what looks like a large conference room. You see one of the soldiers salute and leave the room. Two men, in civilian clothes, remain.

"So this is the statue I've been hearing so much about, Crossley," says the shorter man.

"That's right, Colonel Himmer."

"Are the gold objects still inside?" asks Himmer.

"Everything was removed at the warehouse," Crossley answers.

"You are sure they are worth millions?"

"At least," says Crossley. "But that's chicken feed compared with what we'll get when we find the location of Siling-La."

The door behind Crossley opens and a figure in uniform comes in.

"The men at the airfield are ready for inspection," he says, saluting.

The three men leave the room. You are tempted to get out of the statue now. But would it be safer to wait until it gets dark? Especially since the mansion and grounds seem to be overrun by soldiers.

If you decide to get out of the statue now, turn to page 91.

If you decide to wait until it gets dark, turn to page 29.

"Really?" You try to sound bored. "What *do* you think I am?"

"That I cannot say as yet," replies Singh, "but before this trip is over I will find out."

As soon as the plane lands in Delhi, you are surrounded by Crossley's men again. You all pass through customs and, before you know it, you're in another limousine and threading through the crowded streets of Delhi. The limo stops in front of a large white marble building.

Singh ushers you inside. "We will be here for a few days," he explains. "Then we will go north to the mountains. You will have no need to leave this house."

With that Singh pushes you into a room. You don't have to try the doorknob to know that you're locked in. There is a large couch in the corner. You lie down and are asleep almost immediately.

When you wake, it is dark. Immediately you sense that there's someone else in the room. It takes you a few seconds to recognize Singh.

"We must talk very softly," he whispers. "Careful, I am still not sure if I can trust you."

"If *you* can trust *me!*" you whisper back.

"Yes," Singh says. "I, too, am not what I seem. I am actually an agent for the international police. Crossley is an evil man and must be stopped. But now I must know why you are here."

*If you decide to tell Singh the truth,
turn to page 36.*

*If you decide to stick to your story,
turn to page 112.*

24

"You must leave before dawn tomorrow," says Kando. "You must get a good start in case someone comes after you. Be ready when I tap three times at the door."

Kando leaves, and you, Sylvia, and Jimmy settle down to dinner.

"I wish I knew what this was all about," Jimmy says.

"I'm trying to sort everything out myself," you say. "Your father and his men seem to be a big part of the problem."

"Mr. Crossley isn't my real father," Jimmy says. "My mother married him a year ago, just before she died. My real father died when I was a baby."

You spend the rest of the afternoon talking, then doze off as the sun sets. Before you know it, there are three gentle taps at the door.

Turn to page 63.

"Sylvia Morrison!" you exclaim.

Himmer herds Sylvia toward the truck at gunpoint. She's obviously a prisoner too. Himmer orders you out of the truck, but when he sees Jimmy his expression changes.

"Jimmy Crossley, what are you doing here?"

"Right, Himmer, it's me—and you're going to get it when my father hears about this," Jimmy says.

Himmer laughs. "You think your father cares what happens to his meddling stepson? And where is von Kamp? I don't see him."

The men who captured you look confused.

"I told you to kidnap von Kamp!" shouts Himmer. "And what do you bring me—Crossley's son and . . . who is this?" he says, looking at you.

"This is my friend," Jimmy says.

Himmer turns away in disgust. He goes over to his men and starts yelling and waving his gun in the air. His back is to you, and the other men are only looking at Himmer.

Suddenly, you get an idea. The keys to the truck might still be in the ignition. If you could get into the cab of the truck and get it started . . .

On the other hand, if Himmer or one of his men catches you, it could be your last move.

If you decide to try to start the truck, turn to page 52.

If you decide that going for the truck is too dangerous, turn to page 33.

"Jimmy!" you shout over the street noise.

Jimmy runs toward you. "Quick!" he says. "Two of my father's men are after me. I just gave them the slip."

You launch into the mob on the street, pulling Jimmy along with you. After a few blocks you actually manage to find a taxicab and give the driver von Kamp's address.

Otto von Kamp lives on the ground floor of a new housing project. You and Jimmy walk to the far end of the building and knock on his door. There is no answer. You knock again. Still no answer. You are about to give up when the door opens and a short, bald, heavyset man opens the door part way. There's a gun in his hand—pointed straight at you.

Turn to page 31.

You stay hidden in the statue. Luckily you manage to doze off. Later, you wake up and look out. For a moment you think it's still daylight, but then you realize that bright moonlight is streaming in through the windows of Crossley's conference room.

You feel around for the lever that closed the panel behind you. When you find it and give it a tug, there's a click and a faint scraping sound— and the panel opens. With some difficulty, you manage to climb back out of the statue. Both your legs are asleep and numb. You sit on the floor for a while, rubbing your calves to get the circulation back.

When you can stand again, you walk over and look out the window. You're on the second floor of the mansion. Outside the window is a fairly wide ledge. Carefully you climb out onto it. At the corner of the building you see a drainpipe going down to the ground. All the windows between you and the pipe look safely dark, so you start to work your way along the ledge toward it. Suddenly, as you pass one of the windows, you hear a soft "psst!"

Turn to page 8.

"What do you want?" he demands.

You explain that you are looking for information about Siling-La and that you will gladly pay him for it.

"You seem to be honest. Come in, and sorry about the gun," says von Kamp, putting it away sheepishly. "I'm a little nervous today. So many people want to know about Siling-La."

"Who else has asked about it?" you say.

"A man was here only a couple of hours ago," answers von Kamp. "I think his name was Himmer. He wanted to know exactly where it was."

"Did you tell him?" Jimmy asks.

"I'm not telling anyone," says von Kamp, starting to pace back and forth in front of the window. "I have sworn never to tell."

"About what?" you ask.

"About—" von Kamp starts to say. But before he can finish, there is a swish in the air outside. Von Kamp gives a cry as a knife embeds itself in the window frame, inches away from his head. You manage to catch him as he faints.

If you jump out of the window and go after the attacker, turn to page 38.

If you try to revive Mr. von Kamp, turn to page 107.

"I don't," Sylvia replies. "I'd never even heard of Siling-La before Crossley asked me to help him find it."

At a crossroad you see a sign pointing toward Agra.

"Agra!" Sylvia cries. "That's where the Taj Mahal is, and also where friends of mine live. Head that way."

Soon you see the dome and towers of the Taj Mahal rising like a mirage in the distance. It is incredibly beautiful.

Turn to page 74.

You decide to forget about the truck and wait while Himmer argues with his men. Finally, he orders you, Sylvia, and Jimmy to board the helicopter. You all climb in, followed by Himmer and one of the soldiers. The helicopter lifts into the air and heads north into the mountains. Hours later, it sets down in the central square of a small village.

You, Sylvia, and Jimmy climb out of the helicopter just as a squad of villagers rushes out to refuel it with jerricans of gasoline.

While the villagers work, Himmer marches the three of you into a small house. "I'm leaving for a while," he says, "but I'll be back. In the meantime, no tricks, or you'll pay for it."

Turn to page 81.

Although you're tempted to ask McElroy for help, you want to find out more about Crossley. There's more to his interest in Siling-La than the bet with Buckingham. You wave to Inspector McElroy and keep going to the gate.

Air India flight 10, with you aboard, takes off. Fortunately, you get to sit with Jimmy, though Singh is sitting directly behind you and more of Crossley's henchmen are just across the aisle. It is to be a long flight—you won't get to Delhi until the next morning. You and Jimmy talk about sports until you are sure that Singh and the others have lost interest in your conversation.

"Have you ever heard your father mention a place called Siling-La?" you whisper.

"Oh yes, quite often," Jimmy answers.

"Has he ever said anything about levitation?"

"No, I don't think I've ever heard—"

Jimmy stops in midsentence as you both look up. Singh is bending over you, a fierce expression on his face.

"Sahib Jimmy will sit in the other seat," Singh orders. "I will sit here."

Reluctantly, Jimmy moves. You and Singh sit without speaking for a while. Finally, you break the silence.

"Mr. Crossley seems to have his own private army," you start. Singh doesn't answer. "I guess he feels that he needs a lot of protection with all his money and—"

"Quiet," Singh interrupts. "I do not think you are what you pretend to be."

Turn to page 23.

"Yes," says von Kamp, "into Nepal. There's a small airfield, run by a friend of mine, not far from the border. We may be able to get to Siling-La the easy way."

"Then you know where it is?" asks Jimmy.

Von Kamp pulls out a folded piece of paper from his shirt pocket. It's brown with age and crumbling at the edges. You recognize it at once. "Here is a map I've saved all these years—the top half of it, anyway. Someone else, years ago, got the bottom half, but this is the half that shows the location of Siling-La."

Turn to page 67.

"Okay," you say to Singh, "I'll tell you all I know—which isn't much."

First, you tell Singh about the levitation bet and the map that Mr. Buckingham was going to give you. You also tell him what you overheard in Crossley's conference room.

"It seems to me that what is important is the location of Siling-La. The matter of levitation, true or not, is just a smokescreen," says Singh. "Crossley has been searching for Siling-La for over a year. He has raised a small army to overpower it when he finds its exact location. He has a large transport plane hidden in the foothills of the Himalayas, ready to carry his paratroopers."

"Then levitation really has nothing to do with this whole thing," you say. "The bet was just to make Buckingham reveal his map or somehow lead Crossley to Siling-La."

"Exactly. I must stay in this building and keep a close watch on what is going on. But you can contact a source that I know of here in Delhi."

"Sure," you say. "If I can get out of here."

"That is easy," says Singh. "There is a secret passage out of this chamber. Come, we must hurry."

Turn to page 50.

Snide sits there for a moment, his mouth hanging open. "No, I can't help you," he says abruptly. "Can't you see I'm busy here?"

You certainly are surprised by his sudden change in tone.

"Well, please think it over," you say. "And just in case, here's my phone number."

"All right, leave your number," Snide says. "Now, if you don't leave, I'll have to summon a guard and have you escorted from the museum."

"You know about Siling-La, don't you?" you say. This is a wild guess on your part. You have no idea why Siling-La should be so important. So the monks can levitate themselves—so what! It might make a first-rate circus act, but why should anyone except Buckingham and Crossley care? Could Snide know about the bet, and if he does, why is he so upset about it?

Snide doesn't answer, but you can see that he is shaking. Also, his hand is moving to a button on the side of his desk.

"Okay, okay, I'm going," you say, putting your hands up in mock surrender.

You take one look back as you go down the hall. You can still see Snide through the door, his eyes blazing—but with what? Anger, or fear?

Turn to page 86.

You and Jimmy leave von Kamp on the floor and jump through the window. You find yourselves in a narrow alleyway. A dark silhouette is running toward the street. You try to catch up with it, but before you can, other figures spring out in front of you. You see the glint of the long knives. You turn to run in the other direction, but yet more figures have blocked off that way.

"Looks like they've got us," Jimmy says in a shaky voice. "What do we do now?"

Before you can answer, a rasping voice comes from behind you. "March!" it orders.

Turn to page 47.

At the travel bureau you explain that you want to go to Tibet as soon as possible.

The travel agent checks her computer, then says, "You can get a flight to Peking tomorrow, and go on to Tibet with a tour group from there. In Peking you'll have to pass a physical. They check your blood pressure and that sort of thing, because the altitude in Tibet is very hard on your heart and lungs."

You pay for the tickets, then head for your apartment, stopping to put Mr. Buckingham's check in your safety deposit box. You decide that you'll just pack and sleep when you get home. Someone can come in to clean up the apartment while you're gone.

The next morning it's on to the airport.

Go on to the next page.

Seventeen hours after boarding a China Airlines jet, you land at the Peking airport. There you pass your physical with no trouble and switch to a smaller plane for the flight to Tibet.

You look over the other passengers. Most are Tibetans going home or Chinese officials returning to their posts in Lhasa, the capital of Tibet.

A Tibetan with a shaved head and wearing an orange robe—evidently a monk—takes the seat next to yours. Maybe you can ask him about Siling-La during the flight. On the other hand, you remember what happened with Snide at the museum. It might be better not to ask any questions until you've had a chance to do some research in Tibet.

If you decide to ask the monk about Siling-La, turn to page 64.

If you decide to keep quiet until you get to Tibet, turn to page 117.

You find the piece of paper with Lobsang's address. Next to the address Lobsang has drawn a simple map. You have no trouble finding his house.

"I'm sorry to bother you so soon," you say.

"No need to apologize," says Lobsang, gesturing for you to enter his house. "In fact, I was hoping that you would come soon. I want to tell you about Siling-La."

"Do you know where it is?" you ask.

"There are many who would like to know where it is," he says, dodging the question.

"I didn't know levitation was so popular," you say.

"It's not levitation they're after," says Lobsang. "It's treasure."

"Treasure?"

"Yes," replies Lobsang, "if the legend is true. When I tell you about it, you may not believe me."

Turn to page 56.

You dash up the trail. Bullets hit the ground right behind you. Then you dive behind a rock—just in time.

The machine gun in the helicopter swings back toward Jimmy and the waving hat. For a moment, the pilot tries to head toward two targets at once. He miscalculates and swings the helicopter to the side a fraction of a second too late. You hear one of the chopper's rotors ping against the edge of the ridge. The helicopter does a sudden flip in the air and smacks into the side of the steep hill. There is a tremendous explosion, and a huge fireball plummets down along the face of the cliff into the canyon. A cloud of oily smoke rises into the suddenly silent air.

The three of you walk to the edge of the ridge, staring down as the wreckage of the helicopter burns itself out.

Turn to page 51.

The next day, when you're feeling better, you go out to Buckingham's place. His butler refuses to answer any of your questions. You go home and wait. Every once in a while you try to get Sylvia Morrison on the phone. No luck. Your first case seems to have closed itself. Then one day you see a news item in the paper.

NAJIBABAD, INDIA, APRIL 25.

Hubert Crossley, an American millionaire, was arrested here yesterday with a large paramilitary force, which he had brought secretly into India from the United States. The U.S. government has denied all knowledge of Crossley's activities. Crossley claims that he was searching for the legendary monastery of Siling-La in northern Tibet, but was unable to explain why a large armed force was necessary for his expedition. Indian authorities say Crossley will be dealt with harshly. In a related matter, American anthropologist Sylvia Morrison, who had apparently been held captive by Crossley, was freed.

The End

You go back to sleep and wake up just in time to meet Snide. At the Lunchbox restaurant you take a window table and wait. Snide is late. After a while you order soup. Later, you order a cheese sandwich. You check your watch. It's twelve thirty-five. Well, you think to yourself, I'll wait a bit longer. You eat dessert.

By one o'clock it's clear that Snide isn't going to show up, so you cross the street to the museum and head for the Tibetan collection. Snide isn't there.

"Mr. Snide didn't come in today," one of the guards volunteers. "It must be his day off."

There is something fishy about this whole thing, you think. You have an uneasy feeling. Some sixth sense tells you to get back to your apartment—fast.

Turn to page 65.

Gradually, the monastery becomes opaque again, and the lamas settle back to earth. You open your eyes. You are back in the meditation chamber of the Chetrapa monastery. But you blink in surprise. The lama is floating about a foot off the floor in front of you, his eyes still closed. He settles gently to the floor. Then he leads you back to where Mei Li is waiting. He says something to her and disappears back into the monastery.

"I don't understand that at all," says Mei Li. "He says that you have received the transmission, and that you have only to meditate in total concentration on the image of Siling-La to accomplish your goal."

But the message is clear to you. You know that when you return to the States, you will be able to levitate at least once—enough to save Mr. Buckingham's fortune.

The End

At the same time you see an open truck backing up to the end of the alleyway. When you reach the end of the alley, you're shoved roughly into the truck and pushed to the floor. A canvas cover is thrown over the two of you, and the truck starts off.

You and Jimmy are forced to lie in the truck for hours. Just before dawn, it stops somewhere in the countryside. Someone takes the canvas off and lets you sit up. The sun rises, hot and blistering. Flat brown fields, broken here and there by patches of green, stretch endlessly in every direction. There is an unearthly silence.

You and Jimmy sit for what seems like hours in the hot, breathless air. Then, far off at first, you hear the throbbing of a plane—no, a helicopter. It starts as a speck in the pale, shimmering sky and grows larger and larger until it lands a few hundred feet from the truck.

A woman gets out of the helicopter, her back toward you as she climbs down. A man holding a gun follows her. You recognize the man immediately: Colonel Himmer. It's a few seconds before you recognize the woman.

Turn to page 26.

For the next few days, you, Sylvia, and Jimmy continue toward the village. The trail is even worse than you imagined. Sometimes it leads down into steaming valleys where the vegetation is so thick you can barely push your way through. The worst part is the long black leeches that cling to your legs. You pull them off, leaving bloody sores on your flesh. The mosquitoes and other biting insects are almost as bad. You have big welts all over your body. And all this with the snow of the distant Himalayas in plain sight.

On the higher trails, sudden hailstorms threaten to sweep you off the mountainsides or batter you into unconsciousness with hailstones the size of golf balls. You spend the nights shivering even though you are tightly wrapped in your blankets. By the fifth day you are hiking in shoes cut to pieces by the sharp stones on the trail.

Then you hear the unmistakable sound of a helicopter. It must be Himmer! Instinctively, the three of you hit the ground just as the helicopter appears over a nearby ridge. Quickly you look around for a place to take cover. There's a shallow ditch nearby that might give you some protection. Back down the trail is a large rock formation. It would give you better cover, but you would be exposed for about a minute before you got to it.

*If you decide to hide in the ditch,
turn to page 66.*

*If you decide to run back down the trail to the
rocks, turn to page 89.*

You follow Singh through a panel in the wall, then down a spiral stairway, and finally through a long passageway that leads to the back of a carpet shop.

"Here are some rupees and the address of the German," says Singh, handing you an envelope.

"The German?"

"Yes," says Singh, "his name is Otto von Kamp. If my guess is correct, he is one of the Germans that your Mr. Buckingham followed into Tibet. He may be able to help us find Siling-La before Crossley does. Good luck."

Singh vanishes back into the passageway.

The street outside is filled with a swirling mob of people. You are about to leave, but there by the door is someone you recognize.

Turn to page 27.

"I wonder if Himmer was aboard," Jimmy says.

"I didn't get a close look at the helicopter," you say. "I was too busy keeping my head down."

Then you hear a groan beside you.

"I've been hit!" Sylvia moans. There is a big gash on her lower leg.

"Looks as if you were cut by a fragment of flying rock," you say. You bandage her leg with strips of cloth.

"You and Sylvia stay here and rest," you say to Jimmy. "I'll go on ahead to the village and bring back help. It can't be far now."

"I can keep going," Sylvia insists. "We shouldn't separate."

If you insist that they wait for you while you go on ahead, turn to page 111.

If you decide that you all should go on together, turn to page 59.

52

You spring into the cab of the truck and slam the door. The ignition key *is* still in its slot. As you turn the key the truck springs to life and shoots forward. Himmer whirls around and tries to fire, but the soldiers he was arguing with knock him over in their sudden rush for the truck. They try to jump on the back, but you are already moving too fast.

The truck smashes into the helicopter with terrific force, snapping off the landing gear and sending the cabin tumbling over the ground in front of you. The heavy-duty truck is still moving. You swerve around and head back toward Jimmy and Sylvia. You stop for a split second to let them jump aboard, then floor the accelerator, leaving Himmer and his men behind in a cloud of dust.

"How do you know who I am?" asks Sylvia, as you head down the road toward Delhi.

"You may not remember, but I called you a few days ago about levitation," you say.

"I remember that," says Sylvia. "I was packing, but I didn't make the trip I was planning. They kidnapped me and flew me over here. Himmer thinks I know where this Siling-La place is."

"Do you?" you ask.

Turn to page 32.

"I guess we'll give the ropes a try," you say.

Jimmy and Sylvia agree. Sylvia goes first. She makes it look easy—holding onto the top rope with her hands and sliding her feet along the bottom one. But as soon as you start across the ravine, you realize that it isn't that easy. When you're halfway over, your feet slip off the bottom rope completely. You hang on for dear life before your feet find the rope again. Somehow you make it.

You're worried about Jimmy, but he seems confident, and Sylvia is shouting encouragement to him. He's almost across when he loses the bottom rope and can't find it again. For a moment, he just hangs there. Then he pulls himself the rest of the way, hand over hand, to the ledge. He's a bit shaken but smiles bravely.

The three of you keep going until you reach a high point on the trail. There you rest for a while. Looking back, you can see the thin thread of trail winding along the mountainside. You can even see the rope bridge, far back along it. There are no signs of pursuit.

"I guess we're safe for a while," you say.

"Nothing to it," Jimmy says.

"That may be true," says Sylvia, "but from what I know about these mountains we've only traveled over the easy part."

Turn to page 48.

"Do you know who Genghis Khan was?" asks Lobsang.

"I think so," you answer. "Didn't he conquer most of the world?"

"That's right," Lobsang says. "His Mongol armies conquered—and looted—almost the entire known world of the thirteenth century, from China through the Middle East to central Europe. They took everything they found: gold, jewels, and priceless art. All of this was sent back to Karakoram, the capital city of Mongolia. There, the treasure was said to fill a thousand tents.

"Later, after Genghis's death, his grandson Kublai Khan became emperor of China. Kublai made Peking his capital and sent for the treasure. It never arrived. So Kublai sent an army to Karakoram to sack the city and capture the treasure. But the treasure was gone. Some say it was moved by an immense caravan that took it beyond the Gobi and Taklamakan deserts . . . to the northern part of the Tibetan plateau."

"To Siling-La?" you ask.

"There are those who think so," Lobsang says. "Even today they search for Siling-La—to gain the treasure of Genghis Khan. Now you, too, want to go to Siling-La."

"I was sent here to find it," you say, "but not for treasure. I'm looking for the monks there or someone who can levitate."

Go on to the next page.

"If levitation is your goal, you can stay here and study Tibetan yoga with me," says Lobsang. "In time, you may learn to levitate yourself. If you cannot, I will return with you to the States and prove that it can be done. On the other hand, the dangers of going to Siling-La are greater than you realize. You may find it, but it is not certain that you will return. If you feel you must go to Siling-La, then I can send you to the monastery at Chetrapa. It is said to be the first step on the road to Siling-La. The choice is yours."

If you decide to stay in Lhasa and study with Lobsang, turn to page 96.

If you decide to go to the monastery at Chetrapa, turn to page 90.

"I think if you get a search warrant and raid his warehouse, you'll find a lot of illegally imported merchandise," you tell Inspector McElroy.

The next day, McElroy takes your advice. The police find millions of dollars worth of smuggled art.

"If Crossley can't explain where he got all that stuff," McElroy tells you later, "he's in big trouble."

But when the police go to Crossley's estate to question him, they find it deserted.

"Don't worry," says McElroy. "When Crossley gets back, we'll nab him."

But Crossley never returns. And when you call Mr. Buckingham you find that he's also disappeared. So much for the levitation bet—and your first case.

The End

Sylvia *can* walk with help, so you and Jimmy take turns supporting her. You make slow progress, but you keep going. Finally you reach the village.

Luckily, there's an American mission with a short-wave radio transmitter in the village. They send a message for you to the Indian authorities, who relay it to INTERPOL. Anxiously you wait for a reply. Two days later, a personal message from Singh comes in, thanking you for your help. The message continues:

> *Crossley and his commandos arrested by Indian army for unauthorized military operations. Attack on Siling-La stopped. Not sure if Crossley had found its true location. In any event, Siling-La will be safe for a while, or at least until Crossley gets out of prison, which won't be for a long time.*

The End

Kurt helps you pack his jeep with supplies. Then you, Jimmy, and von Kamp start off into the mountains. Von Kamp looks at his map and is convinced that the jeep can get close enough to Siling-La for you to go the rest of the way on foot. On the third day, the weather turns rainy and cold. Then, up ahead in the road, there is a large new sign. Von Kamp reads the strange script.

"It says that because of the recent rains, the road ahead is very dangerous. There are landslides," he translates.

You all agree that you have no choice but to go on. You drive around the sign. The jeep is the only vehicle on the muddy road. An hour later, as you round a curve at the foot of a steep hill, you hear a rumbling above you. You look up and freeze with terror. The sky is black with enormous boulders hurtling down at you. Von Kamp puts the jeep in reverse, but it is no use. Seconds later you are buried under tons of rock.

The End

Outside, it is still dark. Kando doesn't say a word, but gestures for you to follow. You can barely see her in the darkness. You, Sylvia, and Jimmy follow silently.

Kando leads you down a long hill and away from the village. At the bottom she stops and whispers, "Goodbye and good luck." Then she disappears back into the darkness.

You can sense rather than see the trail. For a while it is level, then it begins to wind steadily upward. The first light of dawn creeps through the ravines around you.

The trail narrows until it becomes a ledge cut into the side of the mountain, with a drop of hundreds of feet below you. You dare not look down, but start counting a hundred steps at a time to take your mind off the precipice.

Then suddenly, up ahead, the trail continues in the form of two frail-looking ropes strung across a ravine and swaying gently in the wind.

"I've crossed this kind of bridge before," says Sylvia. "One rope is for your feet and the other is for your hands. Do you want to try it?"

"We could leave the trail and work our way down to the bottom of the ravine and cross it that way," you say. "That looks just as dangerous, though."

If you decide to cross on the rope bridge, turn to page 54.

If you decide to go down into the ravine, turn to page 70.

64

You turn to the monk and ask, "Do you speak English?"

The monk laughs. "I do. My name is Lobsang. I see that you are American—a tourist?"

"Not exactly," you say. "Actually, I'm looking for a place called Siling-La."

Lobsang gives a momentary start. Then he looks at you with a puzzled expression.

"Siling-La," Lobsang repeats. "What is it you hope to find there?"

"The secret of levitation, or at least whether or not levitation really exists," you answer.

"In that case, I definitely can help you. If you will visit me at my home in Lhasa, I will tell you about Siling-La." Lobsang hands you a slip of paper with his address.

Turn to page 85.

When you get back to your apartment you find the door wide open. That's strange. You're sure you locked it. Cautiously, you switch on the light—then stop, paralyzed by what you see.

The whole place has been ransacked—torn apart. You go through the apartment, turning tables and chairs upright again. Somebody was looking for something. In the bedroom all the dresser drawers have been pulled out, their contents dumped on the floor. Your papers are scattered everywhere. Luckily, you find your passport.

At least you still have Buckingham's check in your pocket—and the map! Maybe that's it, you think. Someone, maybe Crossley, was searching for Buckingham's map of Siling-La. There certainly seem to be a lot of people hung up on levitation.

Then another thought occurs to you. Maybe Snide purposely got you out of the way so he could search your apartment. Could he be working for Crossley? Maybe you should go over to Snide's apartment and see if he's there. Then again, maybe Snide had nothing to do with it, and you ought to just follow Mr. Buckingham's instructions and catch a plane for Tibet.

If you decide to go to Snide's apartment, turn to page 102.

If you decide to go to your travel agent and buy a ticket to Tibet, turn to page 39.

"Quick!" you shout. "Let's hide in that ditch over there!"

You all dash across the trail to the ditch and dive into it. You are just in time, as a long, accurate burst of machine-gun fire splatters the trail. Then the helicopter dips back below the ridge. From the direction of its sound, you realize that it's swinging around to come up behind you. You get an idea. You grab a stick and balance your hat on the end of it.

"You and Sylvia stay here and hold this up," you shout to Jimmy, handing him the stick. "I'm going to give them a moving target up the trail."

"But—but—" Sylvia shouts.

"No time to argue," you shout back.

You jump out of the ditch and start to run just as the helicopter zooms up over the opposite ridge.

Turn to page 43.

At an out-of-the-way border post, von Kamp shows the guard some kind of pass and the van is waved through.

The next day, von Kamp pulls up alongside a broad field where a twin-engine plane is parked.

"That's a Fokker 27," says von Kamp, "the most reliable plane ever built."

A man von Kamp's age strides across the field.

"Kurt!" von Kamp shouts. The two men hug each other for a moment.

"What brings you here, old friend?" Kurt asks.

"I need to go into the mountains," says von Kamp. "I must get to the monastery of Siling-La."

Kurt frowns. "I'll be glad to help you, but I must tell you that the flying to the north is very rough and quite dangerous at this time of year."

"It's vital that I get there," says von Kamp. "I must warn them of danger."

"All right, my friend, if you really must go, I will take you. Ah! but I have another idea. My jeep is like a mechanized mountain goat. It is over there, and you are welcome to take it."

"It will be dangerous either way," says von Kamp. "I cannot decide on my own. Perhaps we should take a vote."

If you vote to go by plane, turn to page 113.

If you vote to go by jeep, turn to page 61.

Inside the museum, you check at the information desk. The third floor seems deserted. You enter the large room that houses the Tibetan collection. Its walls are covered with long scrolls that depict the ferocious demons of Tibetan mythology. Life-size statues of meditating Buddhas sit in the center of the room.

Then you notice a small, bespectacled man—the curator, no doubt—hunched over a desk, way off to the side.

"Are you Mr. Snide?" you ask, as you approach him.

"Yes, I am," he answers. He notices that you are looking at the strange book in his hands. "This is a Tibetan book," he says. "The Tibetan script is printed on long sheets of paper, which, when not being read, are kept between thick blocks of wood. This particular one is the *Tibetan Book of the Dead*. It tells you how to come back for your next incarnation—how to be reborn."

"You mean how to come back as an ant or something?" you ask.

"Humph!" exclaims Snide. "It's nothing to make fun of, and if—"

"I'm sorry," you say, holding up your hand. "I'm really here for information."

"What is it you'd like to know?" Snide asks.

"Well, two things. The first is about levitation."

A faint smile crosses Snide's face.

"The second is whether you've ever heard of a place called Siling-La."

This time Snide looks thunderstruck.

Turn to page 37.

The three of you decide not to cross the ropes. Instead you climb down the steep cliff. Below, a narrow river rushes through the bottom of the ravine. It's hard to keep your footing on the face of the cliff. Sometimes the toeholds disappear entirely. You're beginning to wish you'd used the rope bridge.

You reach the bottom first and stand at the edge of the river, wondering how you'll ever get across. The current is too powerful to swim.

Sylvia points out five widely spaced rocks. "Maybe we could use them as stepping stones," she suggests.

You'll try first. You calculate the distance carefully, then jump to the first rock. So far, so good. Taking a deep breath, you leap to the second. But the third rock is glazed with a thin coating of ice. Your feet fly out from under you as you land, and you plunge into the icy torrent. You're swept downstream so quickly that you never have a chance.

The End

Sylvia has a head start and is halfway down the fire escape before you're even out of the window. You scramble down the fire escape into the dark alley behind the apartment building. At the bottom, there is nothing around you but shadows—and silence.

"Sylvia?" you whisper.

"I'm over here," she answers.

You start toward her. Suddenly, in the dim light, you become aware that you are surrounded by shadowy figures carrying submachine guns.

"Get the map," one of them snaps.

Then you hear Sylvia scream, "No! No! I don't have it!"

You move toward her, when two men grab you, push you against a wall, and search you. "This one doesn't have it either," one of them calls out.

"Then finish them off," a harsh voice orders.

"Now wait a—" you start, but you never manage to finish the sentence. A burst of machine-gun fire takes you off the case.

The End

Sylvia Morrison slams the door and stands with her back against it.

"What's wrong?" you ask.

"I just got a phone call warning me that someone's after me."

"You mean trying to kidnap you?"

"It's a long story . . . I'll try to make it short," Sylvia says with a sigh. "I agreed to help a man called Crossley with some research . . . finding this place in Tibet. I took the job before I found out that Crossley is dangerous, *very* dangerous. I found out from my friend Snide at the museum. Snide had been buying Tibetan art from Crossley—before he found out that Crossley was really a smuggler of stolen art. Crossley somehow found out that Snide was wise to him. Now he has Snide terrified. He's threatening to kill him. I'm afraid Crossley's found out that I know about him. Fortunately, I know some people in the underworld. They just warned me to leave."

"Well, let's go," you say.

"I'm afraid to go out," Sylvia says quietly.

"Is there another way out of here?" you ask.

"Only a fire escape in the back."

"In that case," you say, "you take the fire escape. I'll stay here for a while and try to delay anyone who comes."

"It's not safe for you to stay here!" Sylvia says.

If you go with Sylvia, turn to page 71.

If you stay in the apartment until she gets away, turn to page 93.

"I'd like to go to India," you tell Mr. Crossley. "I have too many things to take care of right now, though."

"Very well," says Mr. Crossley, pressing a button on his desk. "You're free to go."

Two of Crossley's men come into the room.

"Jake and Bradshaw here will take you to the gate," Mr. Crossley says.

You walk between them out of the house and down a dirt path through the woods behind the house. It certainly doesn't look like the way out of the estate, and you're getting suspicious.

"What's that?" you ask, pointing toward the mansion.

As soon as Crossley's men turn their heads, you break into a run, racing deep into the woods. Hoping you can outrun them, you push yourself until your legs feel as if they're burning. Suddenly, you hear a sound that makes you stop in terror.

Behind you, you hear the call of a hunting horn and the furious barking of bloodhounds. You break out in a cold sweat as you realize that Crossley's men may have *let* you break away just to hunt you down.

You've always wondered how the fox feels with the hounds chasing it. You're about to find out.

The End

That night you stay with Sylvia's friends, hoping Crossley won't find you and trying to decide if it's safe to go to the police with your story. Luckily, you don't have to. Next day, in the English edition of the local paper, you read that Crossley and his men have been arrested on charges of bringing illegal arms into India. It sounds as if he's going to be in prison for a long time.

Finally sure you're safe, the three of you decide to return to the States. Jimmy goes to live with his mother's sister. She may not be as rich as Crossley, but she's crazy about Jimmy.

Mr. Buckingham is off the hook with his levitation bet, of course. His butler sends you your first big fee as a private investigator.

The End

You follow Snide and watch him enter an apartment building. After a few minutes, the lights go on in a row of windows on the top floor. Ten minutes later, the lights go off. Snide must have gone to bed early.

You check your watch. It's ten o'clock. I hope Buckingham is still awake, you think to yourself. You want to ask him some questions.

You catch a taxicab at the corner and give the driver Buckingham's address. The cab swings out of town and into one of the richer suburbs of the city. It drives through an elaborate gateway and up a long drive to Buckingham's mansion.

Turn to page 80.

Buckingham suddenly looks hopeful. "*You have to go to Tibet, find the valley of Siling-La, and either learn how to levitate yourself or bring back someone who can. I drew a map of Siling-La's location that I will give you if you agree to go.*"

"Why go all the way to Tibet?" you ask. "I've read about spiritual groups here in the city who say that they practice levitation."

"They *say* they can levitate," replies Buckingham grimly, "but they all fail in front of Crossley's scientific panel."

"Then why don't *you* go to Tibet?" you ask.

"No, no. I'm old and tired. I'd never make it. That's why I need you."

"Still, it would save a lot of trouble if we could find someone closer to home," you offer.

"Well, give it a try if you want. Perhaps this will help." Buckingham hands you a newspaper clipping, dated a few days earlier. There's a photo of a woman over a short article:

Sylvia Morrison, the noted anthropologist, has just returned from a trip to India and the Himalayas, where she has been studying the phenomena of mental telepathy and levitation.

Go on to the next page.

"If you will come to my house tomorrow," says Mr. Buckingham, "I'll give you the map and a check to cover your expenses. By the way, you might see a Mr. Snide at the Museum of Natural History. He's the curator of the Tibetan collection."

You shake hands with Mr. Buckingham and show him to the door. "I'm counting on you to help me," he says.

If you decide to call Sylvia Morrison first, turn to page 5.

If you decide to go to the museum first, turn to page 68.

All the men except Joe go off in search of a forklift. Joe is standing just outside the door to the room. You move as quickly and as silently as you can, and duck behind the door just in time. The forklift turns into the room and heads over to the statue. Its bars slide under the idol and lift it into the air. Then the forklift backs out of the room and down the hallway. All the men leave. There is silence again. You wait for ten minutes or so and walk cautiously toward the door at the end of the hall. There is a glass panel in the door. You look out—at the street!

The door opens easily from the inside. You are somewhere in the city's warehouse district. A big truck is turning the corner at the end of the block. You hope that it's Joe and his friends going off with the idol. When you find a cab, you take it directly to the police station. The police listen to your story, but there's not much they can do without evidence of a crime.

As for your suspicions about Sylvia's being kidnapped, the police claim that both Sylvia and Buckingham are out of town and can't be reached. You'll just have to wait until they get back. You have a hunch it'll be a long wait.

The End

"You haven't seen part of a map lying around?" you ask Flitcher.

"Definitely not," Buckingham's butler answers, ushering you toward the door. "I hope you got the information you came for."

You get back in the waiting cab and give the driver your home address.

Just after you get back to your apartment, your phone rings. "Hello, this is Everett Snide, curator of the Tibetan collection. I'm sorry I gave you the brush-off today, but you took me by surprise. I can tell you a . . . a lot of things about what you are looking for."

"I'll be right over," you say.

"Not tonight," says Snide. "I'll meet you at the Lunchbox restaurant across the street from the museum. Be there tomorrow at noon." There is a click as Snide hangs up.

Didn't even say goodnight, you think to yourself.

You go to bed and doze off right away, but you sleep restlessly. When your alarm rings at eight the next morning you're still groggy. You're tempted to go back to sleep. After all, you don't have to meet Snide until noon. On the other hand, it might be useful to talk to this Sylvia Morrison before you meet with Snide.

If you go back to sleep, turn to page 45.

If you get up and call Sylvia Morrison, turn to page 14.

You ask the cabdriver to wait and ring the bell at the front door. A butler opens it.

"May I help you?" he asks.

You give him your name and ask to see Mr. Buckingham.

"I'm sorry," replies the butler, "but Mr. Buckingham left on a long trip, early this evening."

"That's crazy," you say. "I saw him only a few hours ago."

"He was called away quite suddenly . . . on business."

"What kind of business?" you ask.

"I'm afraid that I'm not at liberty to—" the butler begins. Then he looks at you closely, as if trying to remember something. "What did you say your name was?"

You tell him again.

"Ah! Now I remember. Mr. Buckingham left something for you. Wait, I'll get it."

The butler disappears for a moment and returns carrying a sealed envelope. He hands it to you, and you open it. Inside is a generous check made out to you and signed by Mr. Buckingham. There is also a note:

> *Please report all information about Siling-La to my manservant, Flitcher. Thanking you in advance for your help, Bertram Buckingham.*

There is also a map of northern India, Nepal, and Tibet. At least, there's *half* of a map. The top part has been torn off just above Lhasa, the capital city of Tibet.

Turn to page 79.

The helicopter whines off with Himmer aboard. One of his soldiers remains in the village, guarding the house you're in. The three of you see no one else until that evening when a small, dark-eyed woman arrives with a tray of food. "My name is Kando," she says, placing the tray on a low table. "I do not like what Himmer has done to my village. If you wish to escape, I will help you."

"How long would it take to reach the next village?" you ask.

"Only a few days," Kando replies. "I can get you enough food for the trip."

"Let's go, then," Jimmy says.

Sylvia shakes her head. "That may not be a good idea. I've spent some time in these mountains. They're filled with deep ravines, glaciers, and streams that are impossible to cross. If we stay here, we may be able to foil any plans that Himmer has for us."

If you want to try to escape, turn to page 24.

If you want to stay in the village and try to foil Himmer's plans, turn to page 115.

"The lama said that he will not need a translator. He will communicate with you telepathically—in the realm of universal wisdom beyond words," says Mei Li. "I can't believe that people still believe in those things."

Whatever Mei Li thinks, you follow the lama deep into the monastery to a square hall. In one corner is an altar with a Buddha much like the ones you saw in the museum back in the States. Incense burns in front of it, filling the air with a strange aroma.

The lama gestures for you to sit on the floor in the center of the room facing the altar. He sits in front of you, closing his eyes in deep meditation. You close your eyes, too, and as you do you feel as if you're being transported to a point high above another monastery. Below you are snow-covered mountains, shining with a pure white light. The mountains surround a green park nestled beside a sapphire lake. In the center of the park is the monastery, its gold roof polished to a gleaming brilliance. You can even see the trees in the parks, each one with different-colored blossoms. You don't need to be told that this is Siling-La.

Turn to page 84.

Then you notice that there are lamas meditating cross-legged around the edge of the lake. They look up and see you. Slowly, the lamas begin to rise up off the ground—levitating—still sitting cross-legged, until they form a circle around you in the sky.

You look down and the monastery becomes transparent. Somehow you are able to see right through it. An enormous natural cavern beneath stretches for miles under the earth. And the entire cavern is packed with treasure—treasure the likes of which you never dreamed could exist.

Turn to page 46.

Sometime later, the plane lands in Tibet some sixty miles outside Lhasa, the capital and your destination. A bus takes you down a white sandy road toward the city. Even before you reach Lhasa—from miles off—you can see the majestic white walls and gold roofs of its huge Patala Palace, seemingly floating in the sky ahead.

Soon you enter the old city of Lhasa. Most of the houses in the city are two-story whitewashed structures with flat roofs. But the doorways and windows are gaily decorated with designs of blue, green, and red. Boxes of bright flowers are everywhere.

You check in at the guest house where you are staying. There they give you an "oxygen pillow," with its rubber tube for emergency breathing— just in case you get an attack of altitude sickness.

Maybe you should go right to Lobsang's house. He's your first solid lead to the location of Siling-La and the only person you know in Lhasa. On the other hand, it might be wise to scout around the city and ask a few questions first.

If you decide to go straight to Lobsang's house, turn to page 41.

If you decide to look around Lhasa first, turn to page 94.

You leave the museum and glance at your watch. It's nearly closing time. Perhaps you should wait and see where Snide goes after work. You slip behind a tree across the street from the museum. You watch all of the museum personnel leave—all, that is, except Snide.

Now most of the lights are out in the museum. You wait a while longer, until you start to feel a bit foolish. You realize that the curator could have easily gone out the back door.

You are just about to give up when the museum door opens and someone comes out. Even at this distance you can tell that it's Snide. He looks around as if he thinks he's being watched and then hurries on down the street. Just to be safe, you stay well behind him.

You trail Snide for about a mile. Then he stops suddenly and is joined by another man. You are too far away to see very much, but it looks as if they're exchanging something. The other man hurries away in a different direction. There is something about the new man that makes you want to follow *him*. Either of them might lead you to the answer to the question of why Snide was so upset by the mention of Siling-La. You have to make a quick decision.

If you keep following Snide, turn to page 75.

*If you decide to follow the other man,
turn to page 19.*

You lie on Sylvia's floor, unable to move. Sylvia stands up, pulls off a wig, and throws it on the table. Sylvia is a man. And you recognize him. It's Flitcher, Mr. Buckingham's butler.

"Thanks for making it so easy," Flitcher says. "I'm getting a bonus from Crossley for finishing you off the way I did Buckingham. It's too bad you had to . . ."

But you never hear the rest.

The End

The three of you rush back down the trail toward the rocks. Machine-gun bullets from the helicopter splatter the trail behind you. Panicked, you trip over a small stone and go sprawling.

As you try to get up you look back over your shoulder. The helicopter is so close that you can recognize Himmer leaning out of the cab. There's a demonic grin on his face. You've got to escape him! You're on your feet again, running for the rocks. You almost make it—but not quite.

The End

Lobsang gives you a letter of introduction to the lamas—the monks—at Chetrapa. Just to be on the safe side, you have your trip approved by the authorities in Lhasa. For an extra travel fee, they agree to provide you with an interpreter, a young Chinese woman named Mei Li.

Fortunately, a truck carrying supplies to Chetrapa is scheduled to leave that day. The driver agrees to squeeze you and Mei Li aboard. The truck winds across a wide valley and then north, up into the rolling, golden hills.

It is evening when you finally reach Chetrapa, a small village of squat stone houses grouped around the monastery. You and Mei Li spend the night in separate private homes—the only lodging available.

The next morning, the two of you head up a long flight of stairs to the monastery. One of the older lamas greets you. You give him Lobsang's letter written in Tibetan script. The lama reads it and then speaks to Mei Li.

"He says that if you follow him, he will give you a private audience," Mei Li translates.

As you and Mei Li start to follow, the lama stops and speaks quickly to Mei Li. She stops and stares at him as if not believing what she's just heard.

Turn to page 82.

You climb out of the idol. Cautiously, you go over to the window. Outside, squads of soldiers patrol the grounds.

You look around the conference room. What luck! In one corner is an open box—filled with the uniforms that Crossley's soldiers wear! You try on the one that looks closest to your size. It fits! You look at yourself in a mirror—you're identical to the rest of them out there.

Quietly, you go over to the door and listen. You don't hear anything. You open the door a crack and check out the hallway. Nobody in sight.

You walk along the hallway, down the stairs, and out the front door. Trying not to call attention to yourself, you head for the gate at the far end of the driveway. You're almost there when two of Crossley's soldiers stop you.

"Here, grab this and jump on the truck," one of them orders. He hands you a box and pushes you toward a large brown truck.

Your disguise is a little too good. They think you *are* one of them. You have to do as ordered.

The truck is driven to a small, isolated airstrip far out in the country. Before you know it, you are rushed onto a transport plane.

Buckingham's case will have to wait. You're going to be busy finding a way out of Crossley's "army" and back to the States from India.

The End

Sylvia has just vanished out of the window leading to the fire escape when the door to her apartment crashes in. Two men wearing military uniforms rush inside.

"What is this?" you demand. "There has to be some mistake."

"There's no mistake," one man says, pushing you roughly aside and running to the back window.

They shove you out the front door of the apartment and down the stairs. Outside you see a dark blue limousine parked in front of the apartment house. One of the soldiers—if they are what they seem to be—pushes you against the side of the limousine. The streetlight illuminates the face of the man inside.

"All right, I want Buckingham's map," he says. "No one holds out on Hubert Crossley."

"I don't have Buckingham's map!" you protest.

One of the soldiers jabs you in the side.

"You'd better not have it, then," Crossley warns, "or you're dead."

Crossley's soldiers search you and then jump in the limousine, which speeds off. You lean back against a tree, holding your side. It feels as if a rib has been broken. You're having doubts about this detective business.

Painfully, you hail a cab and climb in. When you get home you call Buckingham's house. You are informed that Mr. Buckingham has left on a trip—a very long trip.

Turn to page 44.

Since Lhasa is the capital of Tibet, you figure there should be a clue somewhere here to the location of Siling-La. First, you explore the narrow streets that twist around the base of the Patala Palace. Later you take the guided tour of the palace and its one thousand rooms, but of course you don't go into every one.

You're about to return to the guest house when you think you recognize a woman ahead of you. You watch her as she enters a small shop, closely pursued by a man. Impulsively, you follow them inside.

The light in the shop is very dim. Someone grabs your arm, and you feel the barrel of a gun poking into your ribs.

"Into the back!" a heavy voice orders.

Turn to page 100.

You stay and study with Lobsang for seven months. Under his strenuous training, you learn things in weeks that might take others years. You are taught the mystic secrets of old Tibet. By the time you are ready to leave, you have mastered the art of complete concentration and are on your way to learning the secrets of mental telepathy. Levitation—well, you're beginning to catch on to it.

It must be the hundredth time you've tried. "Just *concentrate*," says Lobsang patiently. "You can do it."

You try. And you try. Slowly but surely you feel yourself rising up into the air. Not more than a couple of inches—but you've done it!

When you return to the States, the first thing you do is call on Mr. Buckingham. You can't wait to see the look on Crossley's face when you demonstrate levitation. Buckingham's butler answers the door and explains that Mr. Buckingham isn't there and won't be for a long time!

"But I *have* to get in touch with him," you insist. "It's very important."

It's no use. You never hear from Buckingham again. Or anything about Sylvia Morrison or Crossley, either. Oh, well, all the things you learned in Tibet will come in *very* handy in your future investigations.

The End

When you awake you find yourself in a large, elegant room. This must be some kind of mansion, you think. Still a little wobbly, you stand up and find yourself facing a sharp-featured middle-aged man.

"So this is our young investigator," he says.

"Just what's this all about?" you ask in a shaky voice.

"You want to know what this is all about?" The man's voice is furious. "Since you won't be leaving here for a while—if ever—I'll tell you exactly what you're meddling in. I am Hubert Crossley. I import—let's call it that—antique art treasures from the Orient. Just recently I discovered that the finest ones come from a place called Siling-La, somewhere in Tibet. Yet with all my resources I couldn't find its exact location. Then I remembered that old fool Buckingham at the club. He was always telling some wild levitation story, set in a place called Siling-La. He even said he had a map showing its location. First I tried to buy the map from him. He wouldn't sell. So I made that silly bet to smoke him out. Today I thought Buckingham had given the map to you. My men searched you while you were unconscious. Apparently you don't have it—not that it would do you any good now."

Crossley's men take you down to the mansion's basement and lock you in a cell at the end of a long corridor.

You'll be there for a long time—at least until Crossley gets enough money and treasure to satisfy him. And that could take forever.

The End

You're pushed through a curtain. There, sitting behind a small table, is Sylvia Morrison—you recognize her from the newspaper photo—and another man you don't recognize.

"I don't know why you followed me," says the man with the gun, "but since you're here, you may have the honor of joining Ms. Morrison on a little adventure I've planned for her."

You're trying not to look scared, but Sylvia sounds perfectly calm as she says, "You're a fool to think you can get away with this, Crossley."

Turn to page 109.

As you turn the corner you skid to a stop. Five men are coming toward you. You try to jump back before you're seen, but you're not quick enough. You'll have to make a run for it! You tear down the hallway, but you're tackled just before you reach the end. You hit the ground with a thump and lose consciousness.

Turn to page 99.

There's a crowd outside Snide's building, as well as an ambulance and several squad cars.

"What happened?" you ask one of the policemen near the front door.

"This guy Snide jumped out of his window a little while ago," he says. "They're loading him in the ambulance now—but I think they're taking him to the morgue."

A chill runs down your spine. Then you see a familiar figure push his way out of the crowd and start up the street. He looks a lot like Flitcher, Mr. Buckingham's butler.

You take off after Flitcher, but not quickly enough. The butler seems to have vanished. Forget it, you think to yourself. This case is getting complicated—and deadly. Buckingham has left on a long trip. You have *half* a map—the wrong half. And the man who gave it to you, Flitcher, may be a murderer. You're not doing anything until you hear from Mr. Buckingham again *personally*.

But you never do.

The End

"Not much we can do," says Kurt, "except—" He stops speaking and looks off across the snow, shielding his eyes from the glare. "Is that a line of monks walking toward us, or am I already coming down with mountain sickness?"

"They're from the monastery at Siling-La!" von Kamp shouts.

"I don't believe this," Jimmy says.

But von Kamp is right. The monks lead you through a mountain pass to the warm green valley of Siling-La. It feels as if you've just stepped into summer. You know you've never seen a place this beautiful.

The abbot greets you, and you warn him about Crossley and his plans to invade the monastery.

"There is no danger," the abbot says. "Have you ever heard of the *Tibetan Book of the Dead*? It describes the visions you see—hallucinations—as you pass from death to rebirth. Some of these hallucinations are images of horrible demons. These same images protect the monastery. Though they exist only in the mind, they will seem real enough to anyone who tries to attack us."

You're not sure you understand this, or would believe it if you did, so you change the subject. "Did Buckingham know about the treasure?"

"No, he thought levitation treasure enough," the abbot replies. "Now let me show you what you've come so far to see."

Turn to page 105.

Turn to page 17.

"Inspector McElroy," you call out, suddenly breaking away from Crossley's guards. "I'm so glad to see you!"

Crossley's men hesitate for a split second—long enough for you to run to Inspector McElroy's group. You walk along with him, heading toward the exit. Crossley's men look furious.

"Could you give me a lift downtown?" you ask.

"Of course," McElroy says with a smile.

As McElroy drives away you start to tell him about Crossley.

"Strange that I should run into you," says McElroy. "The department has had Crossley under observation for some time now. He's training some kind of private militia out there on his estate. But as long as he stays on his own property there's not much we can do."

"I'm not so sure of that," you say. "I have a suspicion about Mr. Crossley. It might help you get your hands on him."

Turn to page 58.

Gently you shake von Kamp. He groans and stirs. Meanwhile, Jimmy closes the window and checks the front door to make sure it's locked. Only just in time. A moment later there's a pounding on the door. Luckily, von Kamp is coming around.

"Is there any way out of here besides the front door?" you ask.

"I'm afraid not," von Kamp answers. "No, wait! There's a ventilation shaft in the back with a ladder up to the roof."

Von Kamp jumps to his feet and leads the way to the shaft. Quickly he pulls a grille off the wall and squeezes inside. You and Jimmy follow. You climb the three stories to the roof.

"At the other end of the building," whispers von Kamp, "there's an outside stairway to the ground."

Back on the ground, von Kamp leads you through a narrow alley to an beat-up old van.

You all jump in, and von Kamp pulls out into the congested traffic.

"Where are we going?" Jimmy asks.

"Well, first we're going to get out of the city and head north. Eventually we'll reach Siling-La."

For the next few days, you just keep riding—living and sleeping in the back of the van. The broad, dusty plains gradually give way to rolling hills.

"I'm taking a back road," says von Kamp. "It'll be easier to get across the border that way."

"Across the border?" you ask.

Turn to page 35.

"No, Ms. Morrison," Crossley replies. "You're a fool if you think anyone can stop me. It's time to go now."

You and Sylvia are forced at gunpoint into a truck waiting behind the shop. The driver is Chinese. You realize that with the canopy pulled down around the back of the truck it looks just like any Chinese army vehicle.

You ride for an hour. Finally, the truck reaches a field where a transport plane is parked, its engines idling. You and Sylvia are pushed aboard. Crossley follows you inside. The plane is filled with paratroopers.

A soldier sits you down roughly, and the plane takes off. It flies for about half an hour. Your mind is racing, trying to figure out a way to escape, when the paratroopers begin strapping on their chutes. They're preparing for a jump.

You look out of the window. Far below, nestled in the snowy mountains, you see a single patch of green and the glint of a lake.

The paratroopers are lined up by the now open side door. Cold air rushes into the plane. Two paratroopers come for you and Sylvia, shoving you toward the door where Crossley waits.

"I don't want you to miss our attack on Siling-La, so you'll make the first jump. Too bad we don't have extra parachutes for you," Crossley hisses as he pushes you and Sylvia out of the plane and into empty space.

The End

Sure that you'll have no trouble finding the village, you insist that Jimmy and Sylvia wait on the trail. Then you set off at a quick pace.

Hours later, you come to a fork in the road. You have no idea which branch of the trail to take. Perhaps both lead to the village. You don't want to go all the way back to where Jimmy and Sylvia are waiting.

You take the trail on the right. After a while you come to a broad field of ice stretching ahead. You can't see beyond it, but something tells you that the village is just on the other side.

You start across the ice. It looked flat from a distance, but it's actually full of ruts and deep gullies. Soon you find yourself sliding along the bottom of an ice canyon. Shiny walls of ice tower up on both sides of you.

Your hands and feet are numb with cold, but you know Sylvia and Jimmy are depending on you. You force yourself to keep moving. You are almost through the ice canyon when you hear a terrible cracking sound. In a panic, you start to run forward. But it's impossible to keep your footing on the ice. Before you can get through the canyon, its walls of ice collapse on top of you.

The End

"I'm here because I'm Jimmy's friend," you explain.

"All right," says Singh, "if that's the way you want to play it. But if you say anything to anyone about this meeting, we'll both be killed."

You hear the click as a panel in the wall closes—then silence. Singh is gone. The next morning, you examine every inch of the ornate inlaid wall. You can't find a trace of the panel that Singh disappeared into.

Later that day, two of Crossley's men—these ones in civilian clothes—appear at the door. Jimmy is standing between them.

"Mr. Crossley says that he is far too busy here to spend time with you two," one of the men explains. "He's decided to send you on to the south of India. He'll meet you there."

You and Jimmy are taken back to the limousine. Somewhere south of Delhi, you are transferred to a camper bus. It is the start of a completely new adventure. Mr. Crossley was right about one thing, anyway—this trip *will* be educational.

The End

Kurt's plane dashes down the short runway and pulls sharply up into the air. You, Jimmy, and von Kamp hold your breath as the plane narrowly clears the treetops. Then Kurt banks the plane toward the north. Soon you see jagged, snow-peaked mountains in the distance. Before you know it, you are flying between them, the snow glistening white around you. The air starts to get bumpy, and a few dark clouds appear ahead.

"It's going to be rough flying from now on," warns Kurt. "And you'll have to give me directions from here."

Von Kamp pulls out the map and tries to get his bearings from the nearby peaks.

"It shouldn't be too far," he says. "We're well into Tibet. According to this map, we should be heading right for the monastery."

However, you fly on for what seems like a long time.

"Can't go much farther," says Kurt. "My gas is at the point of no return—soon there'll be just enough fuel for the return flight."

"It should be somewhere just ahead," says von Kamp, peering at his map and then out the window.

You look out too, but can't see anything except mountains and snow. Then you think you see a tiny patch of green up ahead—but you're not sure.

Suddenly, both the engines of the Fokker start to sputter and then die completely.

Turn to page 116.

The three of you agree to stay in Kando's village. While Himmer is gone, you convince the villagers that you are an American millionaire, which isn't hard, since they're ready to believe that all Americans are millionaires. You promise to pay the villagers more than Himmer is paying them if they'll help you. They grab Himmer's guard and lock him up.

When Himmer and his men return in the helicopter a week later, they, too, are seized and locked up.

Fortunately, Sylvia has a pilot's license, so she has no difficulty taking you and Jimmy back to Delhi in the helicopter. There, you find that Crossley has been arrested by the Indian police. Jimmy feels sorry for his stepfather, but also relieved that the takeover of Siling-La has been stopped.

You, Jimmy, and Sylvia spend another month in India on vacation. During that time you find a yogi who seems to be able to levitate—or at least no one can prove he is faking. You talk him into coming back to the States, just in case Crossley gets out of jail and wants to claim his bet with Buckingham.

The End

116

"I don't understand it!" exclaims Kurt. "We have enough fuel. Can't seem to get the engines started again. Looks like we're going down."

Kurt is an experienced mountain pilot. He somehow manages to miss the side of a nearby mountain and then skid the plane in on the only level piece of snow in that part of Tibet. The plane lands with a jarring crunch in the side of a huge snowbank. You all climb out somewhat dazed.

"What do we do now?" you ask.

Turn to page 103.

You stay silent during the flight to Tibet. The monk looks at you every once in a while and smiles, almost as if he could read your mind.

When you arrive in Lhasa, you check into the guest house with your tour group and then get to work. You hire an interpreter and ask everyone who will listen if they have ever heard of Siling-La. No one has. When you ask about levitation, you always get the same answer: "In the old days . . . but now . . ."

Finally your tour group leaves, and you have to leave with it. Back in the States, your first stop is Mr. Buckingham's house.

Flitcher, the butler, answers the door. "Mr. Buckingham is still away," he tells you. "I'm handling all his affairs in his absence."

"I'm afraid I failed," you say. "I came by to return Mr. Buckingham's check."

"Don't worry about the levitation bet. It has been canceled by both Mr. Buckingham and Mr. Crossley."

"You mean my whole trip was unnecessary?" you ask.

"I'm afraid so," Flitcher replies. "But Mr. Buckingham has informed me by phone that you are to keep the check—for expenses and your trouble."

You leave Buckingham's not quite satisfied and more than a little suspicious. But what can you do? And looking back on your trip, it was an adventure and it *was* worth it.

The End

ABOUT THE AUTHOR

RICHARD BRIGHTFIELD is a graduate of Johns Hopkins University, where he studied biology, psychology, and archaeology. For many years he worked as a graphic designer at Columbia University. He has written *Secret of the Pyramids, The Phantom Submarine,* and *The Dragons' Den* in the Choose Your Own Adventure series and has coauthored more than a dozen game books with his wife, Glory. The Brightfields and their daughter, Savitri, live in Gardiner, New York.

ABOUT THE ILLUSTRATOR

PAUL GRANGER is a prize-winning illustrator and painter.

We hope you enjoyed reading this book. If you would like to know more about the Choose Your Own Adventure or Skylark books, or if you have difficulty obtaining any of them locally, or if you would like to tell us what you think of the series, write to:

Choose Your Own Adventure,
Corgi Books,
Century House,
61–63 Uxbridge Road,
London W5 5SA

WHO KILLED HARLOWE THROMBEY?
by EDWARD PACKARD

Millionaire Harlowe Thrombey hired you to find out who was out to get him. But before you even got started, someone laced his bedtime brandy with arsenic. Now you have a murder case on your hands! The suspects include his wife Jane, his nephew Chartwell, and his niece Angela – all heirs to his enormous fortune.

How do you solve this mystery? *If you search for clues in the pantry, turn to page 31. If you follow up on a tip from the gardener, turn to page 48. If you question one of the guests at Thrombey's last meal – the mysterious Dr. Robert Lipscomb – turn to page 28.*

0 553 23181 2   95p

INSIDE UFO 54-50
by EDWARD PACKARD

You're aboard a supersonic jet, high above the Atlantic. Suddenly a huge, gleaming white cylinder shoots out of the clouds. The next thing you know you are inside the galactic ship *Rakma* – captured by the all-powerful A-TY Masters!

How do you escape? *If you pretend to cooperate with these ruthless beings*, turn to page 82. *If you try to sabotage the U-TY computers*, turn to page 108.

Be careful! One choice might lead you back to earth, but another might put you in orbit forever! What happens all depends on the choices *you* make. And the best part is that you can keep reading and re-reading until you've had *many* fantastic adventures!

0 553 23175 8   95p

CHOOSE YOUR OWN ADVENTURE

SKY LARK CHOOSE YOUR OWN ADVENTURE